Vanilla
PREM
2

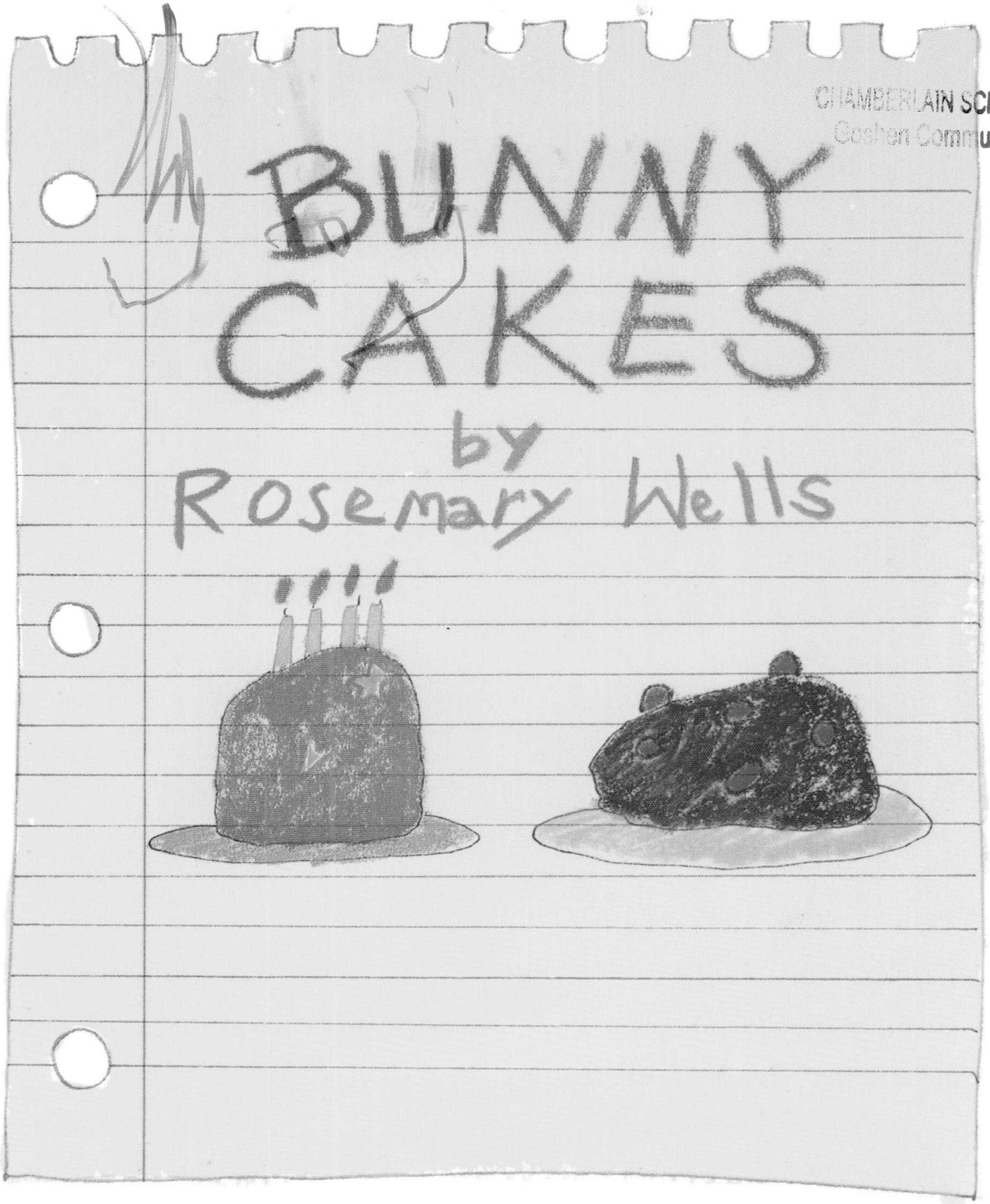

SCHOLASTIC INC.
New York Toronto London Auckland Sydney

For Ann Tobias

ISBN 0-590-03199-6

12 11 10 9 8 7 6 5 4 3 2 1 8 9/9 0 1 2 3/0

Printed in the U.S.A 36
First Scholastic printing, January 1998

The artwork for each picture is an ink drawing with watercolor painting.

It was Grandma's birthday.

Max made her an earthworm birthday cake.

"No, Max," said Max's sister, Ruby. "We are going to make Grandma an angel surprise cake with raspberry-fluff icing."

Max wanted to help.

"Don't touch anything, Max," said Ruby.

But it was too late.
Ruby sent Max to the store
with a list that said:

Max wanted Red-Hot Marshmallow Squirters for his earthworm cake. So he wrote "Red-Hot Marshmallow Squirters" on the list.

The grocer could not read Max's writing.
"Eggs!" said the grocer, and he gave Max eggs.

Max brought the eggs home to Ruby.

"Don't bump the table, Max!" said Ruby.

But it was too late.
Ruby sent Max back to the store with a list that said:

This time Max wrote "Red-Hot Marshmallow Squirters" in a different way.

Max hoped and hoped for his Squirters,

but the grocer still couldn't read Max's writing.

"Milk!" said the grocer, and he gave Max milk.

Max brought the milk home to Ruby.

"There's a yellow line on the floor, Max," said Ruby.

"You can't step over that line."

But Max crossed the line anyway.

Over went the flour.

Ruby got out her pencil.

This time Max wrote "Red-Hot Marshmallow Squirters" in the most beautiful writing he knew.

Max could almost taste the Marshmallow Squirters.

"Flour," said the grocer, and he gave Max flour.

When Max got home, there was
a sign on the kitchen door.
"Max, the kitchen is no place
for you," said Ruby.

Ruby finished up her cake.

She baked it and cooled it and iced it
with raspberry-fluff frosting.
"It needs something else, Max," said Ruby.

"Birthday candles, silver stars, sugar hearts,
buttercream roses," wrote Ruby.
Meanwhile Max had a brand-new idea.

He drew a picture of Red-Hot Marshmallow Squirters on Ruby's list and ran to the grocer. He could not wait.

“Birthday candles, silver stars, sugar hearts, buttercream roses!” said the grocer. “What’s this? Why, it must be Red-Hot Marshmallow Squirters!”

Ruby's cake looked just beautiful.

Max went out and put caterpillar icing on his earthworm cake.

Grandma was so thrilled, she didn't know which cake to eat first.